STEP-BY-STEP

MAKING KITES

DAVID MICHAEL

ILLUSTRATED BY JIM ROBINS

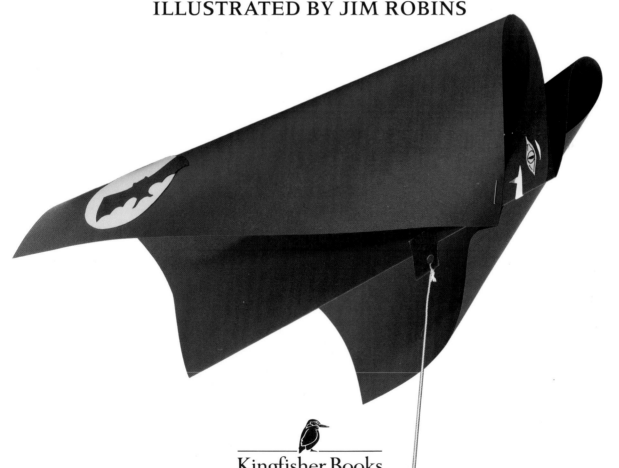

Kingfisher Books

NEW YORK

KINGFISHER BOOKS
Grisewood & Dempsey Inc.
95 Madison Avenue
New York, New York 10016

First American edition 1993
10 9 8 7 6 5 4 3 2 1 (lib.bdg.)
10 9 8 7 6 5 4 3 2 1 (pbk.)

Library of Congress Cataloging-
in-Publication Data
Michael, David.
Making kites / David Michael.
—1st American ed.
p.cm. — (Step-by-step)
Summary: Provides an introduction
to kite construction and directions
for making various kinds of kites,
including a two-stick kite, box
kite, superstunter, and wind sock.
   1. Kites — Juvenile literature.
[1. Kites. 2. Handicraft.]
I. Title. II. Series: Step-by-step
(Kingfisher Books)
TL759.J44 1993
629,133'32 — dc20 92-42913 CIP AC

ISBN 1-85697-923-7 (lib.bdg.)
ISBN 1-85697-922-9 (pbk.)

Designed by Ben White
Illustrations by Jim Robins
Photographed by Steven Sullivan
Cover design by Terry Woodley
Kites built by David Michael and
Anne Bates

Printed in Hong Kong

CONTENTS

To build most of the kites in this book, you will need to buy equipment from a specialist kite or hobby store. You will also need some simple household equipment and a generous working area — kite building takes up a lot of room.

Frame Materials

The *spars* or sticks that make the frame of a kite can be made from a variety of materials.

Bamboo is a traditional material and is still useful for smaller kites.

Wooden sticks can be bought in model and kite shops, as well as hardware stores.

Plastic rods are strong, light, and easily bent. Bigger sizes come in the form of hollow tubes, which reduce the weight.

More expensive, but strongest and lightest sticks of all, are those made from *carbon fiber*.

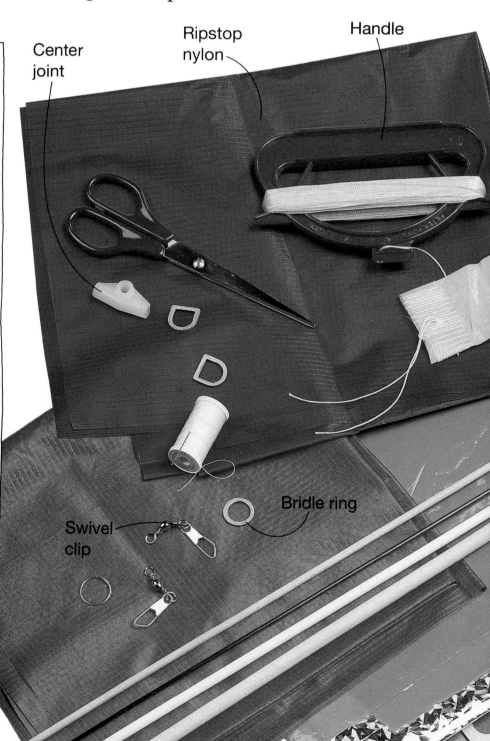

Center joint

Ripstop nylon

Handle

Bridle ring

Swivel clip

4

Sail Materials

The sail of a kite can be made from anything that is light and won't tear easily. Light-wind kites can even be made from *paper*. *Plastic* sheeting is probably the best choice for beginners — it is strong, waterproof, and can be repaired with tape. *Coated ripstop nylon* needs to be sewn rather than taped, but it is the first choice of the experienced kite builder.

Lines and Rings

String comes in many different weights, from thin thread for light kites to super-strong, tough enough to lift you off the ground! For your first kites, buy medium-strength string and a simple plastic handle. Later, you may prefer to use string mounted on a reel. Buy aluminum bridle rings, or use curtain rings. A swivel clip lets you add a spinning tail.

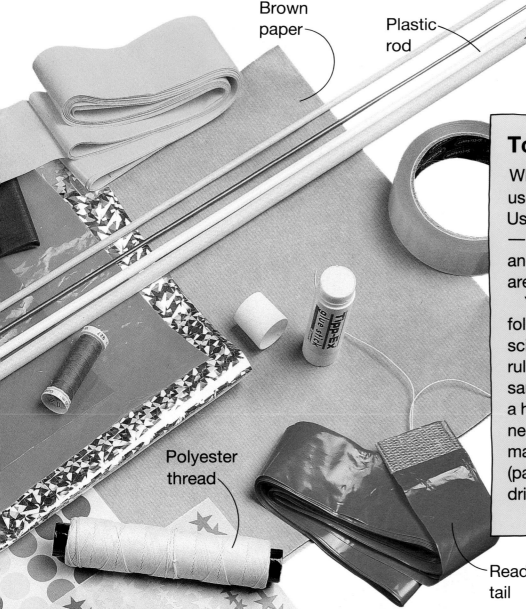

Brown paper

Plastic rod

Carbon rod

Hardwood rod

Polyester thread

Ready-made tail

Tools

White craft glue can be used to glue all kite parts. Use tape when you can — invisible, waterproof, and double-sided tape are all useful.

You will also need the following: a craft knife, scissors, a protractor, ruler, a small hacksaw, sandpaper, a compass, a hole punch, and a needle and thread. To make the Hexafringe (page 35), you will need a drill and an adult's help.

5

PARTS OF A KITE

Although the kites in this book all have different designs, the basic parts share the same name. These parts are shown in the diagrams below. On the following pages, you will find everything you need to know about putting the parts together.

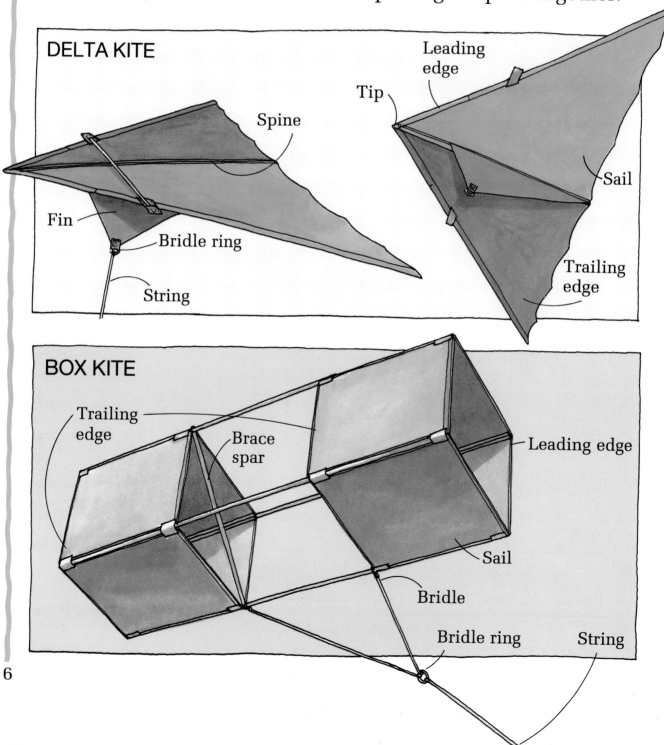

DELTA KITE

Spine

Leading edge

Tip

Sail

Fin

Bridle ring

String

Trailing edge

BOX KITE

Trailing edge

Brace spar

Leading edge

Sail

Bridle

Bridle ring

String

MAKING KITES

Making kites isn't difficult. Follow the instructions carefully, and check your measurements at every stage. If you do, your kites should fly just as well as the ones that we built while making this book!

Making the Frame

To make the spars, cut the dowel, plastic, or carbon rods into lengths with a small hacksaw. Try to keep the sawing even and gradual — if you try to force the spars, they may snap. Use fine sandpaper to smooth the edges of the spar ends.

Joints

To join the spars, you can use strong twine, tape, or glue. For kites with angled sails (for example, the Superstunter on page 30), you will need to buy a metal or plastic bent center joint from a kite store. Plastic joints are rigid, but metal joints can be bent to fit the angle of your kite.

Joining Sails

To join plastic, paper, or cardboard, you can use tape. Overlap materials wherever possible, and tape both sides for extra strength. If you are using ripstop nylon, you should sew the pieces with a needle and thread. Overlap the edges by at least half an inch, and try to make the stitches small and neat. For extra strength, stitch two parallel lines, $\frac{1}{4}$ inch apart.

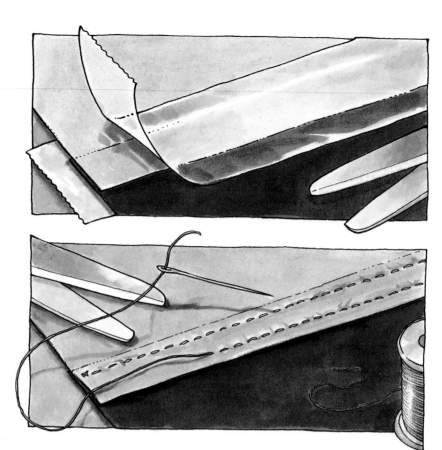

Making Pockets

The spars are kept in place by pockets at the tip, base, and top ends. They are quite simple to make.

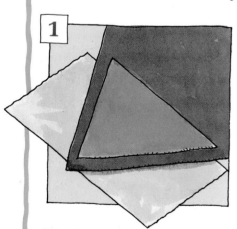

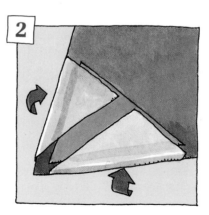

Taping Pockets:
Cut a triangle out of strong plastic to match the corner of the sail of the kite.

Use a strip of tape to attach the triangle to the corner of the sail to make a pocket.

Fold down the tip of the pocket to make a straight edge. Tape in place securely.

Sewing Pockets:

Cut a strip from nylon, $3\frac{1}{2}$ x 1 inch. Fold in half and sew as shown. Lay the pocket over the corner of the sail, so that it overlaps the corner. Sew it to the sail — the x-shaped stitching will add extra strength.

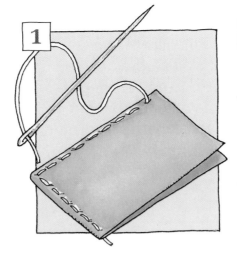

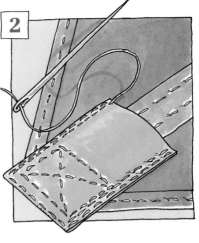

Bridle Ring Pocket:

The Delta kite on page 32 uses a bridle ring pocket. To make it, just follow the stages shown here.

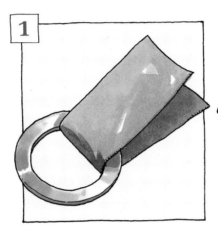

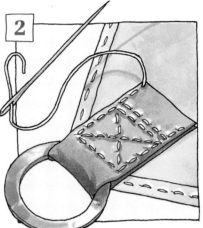

Below: The corner pockets and bridle ring pocket are sewn to ripstop nylon sails, using strong polyester thread.

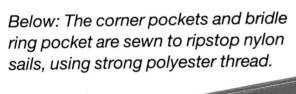

Attaching Strings

When making kites, you will need to use two main strings. The *bridle* is tied to the kite at one end (using a bowline knot) and to a *bridle ring* at the other end (using a lark's head knot). The *string* is then tied to the bridle ring with a bowline knot. These two knots are shown below.

Lark's Head Knot

Bowline Knot

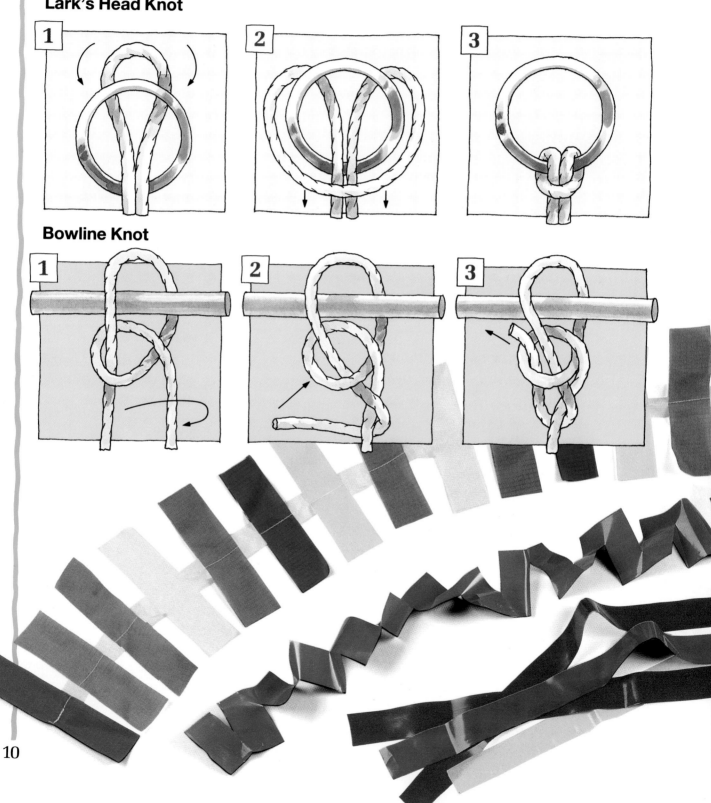

TAILS

Tails are not only colorful and attractive. They have a practical use, too. They make a kite more stable in the air and are essential for many designs, such as the Diamond Two-stick on page 22, and other kites with flat sails.

A simple ribbon tail can be made by cutting plastic or nylon into a long strip, 1 to 2 inches wide.

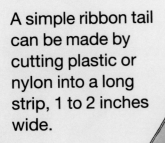

This tail catches more air than a ribbon. Simply cut notches down its entire length with scissors.

Tassel tails are made by joining a group of multi-colored ribbons at the base of the kite.

Streamer tails are fastened, evenly spaced, across the base of a flat kite.

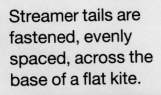

A flat tail uses one single wide ribbon (see the Black Mamba on page 29).

DECORATIONS

For added interest, try making some of the decorations shown here. They add color and stability to the kite, and look spectacular in the air.

Spinning Helix

This kite looks hypnotically attractive as it spins round and round in the wind.

Using a plate as a guide, cut a large circle out of light cardboard or shiny Melinex.

Mark a point $\frac{3}{4}$ to $1\frac{1}{4}$ inches from the edge. Make a slanted cut to form the end of the tail.

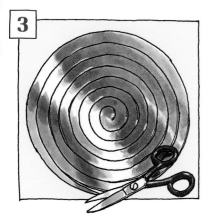

Keep cutting in a spiral until you reach the center. Keep the lines $\frac{3}{4}$ to $1\frac{1}{4}$ inches apart.

Attach the helix to the base of your kite, using a swivel clip (available from a kite shop).

Wind sock

This can be made from nylon, plastic, or (as here) from shiny plastic wrapping paper.

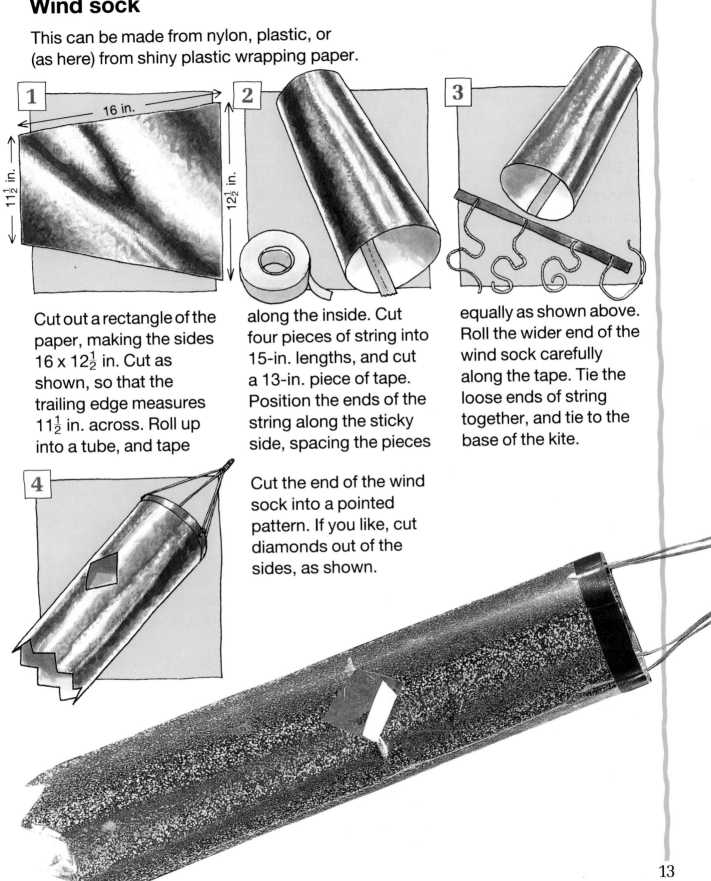

1 16 in. / $11\frac{1}{2}$ in.

2 $12\frac{1}{2}$ in.

3

Cut out a rectangle of the paper, making the sides 16 x $12\frac{1}{2}$ in. Cut as shown, so that the trailing edge measures $11\frac{1}{2}$ in. across. Roll up into a tube, and tape

along the inside. Cut four pieces of string into 15-in. lengths, and cut a 13-in. piece of tape. Position the ends of the string along the sticky side, spacing the pieces

equally as shown above. Roll the wider end of the wind sock carefully along the tape. Tie the loose ends of string together, and tie to the base of the kite.

Cut the end of the wind sock into a pointed pattern. If you like, cut diamonds out of the sides, as shown.

4

Tailspinner

This tailspinner spins around in the wind, sending its ribbons flying through the air.

Making the Tailspinner

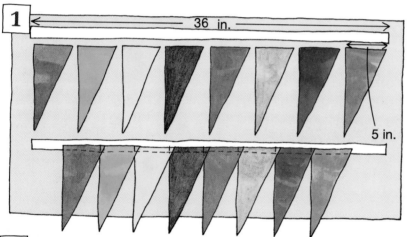

1 Cut eight triangles out of plastic or nylon. Make each triangle about 5 inches on the short end. Cut a band 1 yard in length from ripstop nylon. Sew on the triangles, overlapping each one by $\frac{1}{2}$ inch at the top.

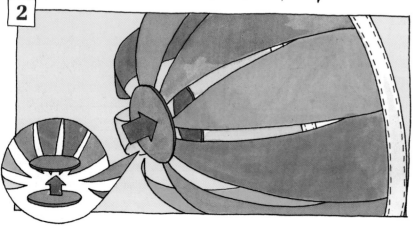

2 Cut two tail disks out of plastic or nylon. Use a compass to make sure they measure $1\frac{1}{4}$ inches across. Glue the tips of the triangles under the tips of one of the circles, then glue the second circle underneath the triangle tips.

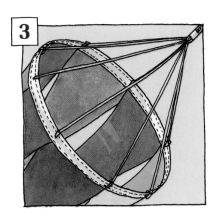

3

Cut eight pieces of kite string, each 10 inches long. Tape them to the band and tie the other ends to a swivel clip.

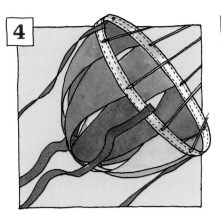

4

Tie or sew on four streamers made from bright pieces of plastic. These whirl around in a spiral.

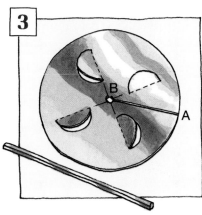

5

Attach the swivel clip to the base of the kite. Or, if you prefer, clip the tailspinner halfway up the kite string.

Climbing the line

When your kite is flying in the sky, what else can you do? Try slotting this little spinner up the line, and letting go. . .

Cut a 4-inch-diameter disk from stiff cardboard. Make a hole (about $\frac{1}{8}$ inch wide) through the center.

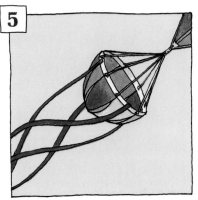

1

Use a compass to draw four $1\frac{1}{3}$ inch circles. Cut out half the circles, and bend up as shown. Cut the line A to B.

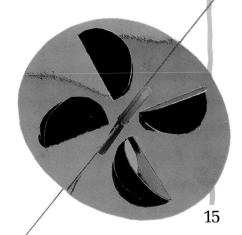

2

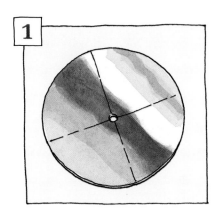

3

Cut a $2\frac{1}{3}$-inch length of plastic straw, and cut a lengthwise slit in it. Glue in the center of the disk at right angles, so that both cuts line up.

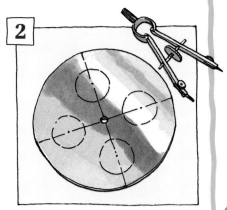

15

FLIGHT TESTING

The test flight is the moment of truth — have you built the kite well? Will it fly, or will it crash? Will it even get off the ground? Hopefully, it will soar like a bird — but you may need to adjust the balance first. Always choose open land to fly in, and don't try to fly the kite in very strong winds or when the air is still.

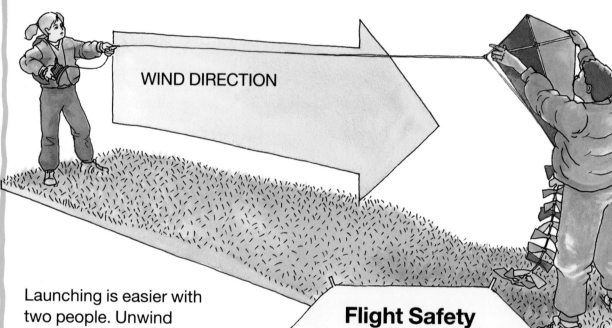

WIND DIRECTION

Launching is easier with two people. Unwind 20-30 feet of string and pull it taut. Make sure that your helper is facing into the wind. He or she should raise the kite into the air, with the kite facing the wind. Pull firmly on the string — the kite should soar up. If it doesn't, try walking backward or give a few sharp tugs on the kite string.

Flight Safety

* Keep away from electricity wires, trees, and houses.

* Don't fly kites near airfields, or at heights which may get in the way of aircraft.

* Use leather gloves if it is very windy. The string can burn the hands if it unwinds suddenly.

* Don't fly in stormy weather. Lightning could strike the kite and kill you.

* Don't launch the kite if people or animals are walking past.

Adjusting the Balance

A kite that flies perfectly one day may fly badly the next time you take it out — this may be due to a change in wind conditions. Try moving the bridle ring.

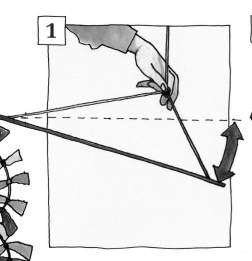

1 Before flight, hold the kite by the bridle ring. Adjust the ring so that the kite hangs at 20-30° into the wind.

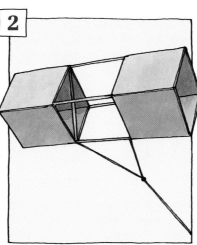

2 Moving the bridle forward makes the kite fly higher, at a flat angle to the wind. This is good for smooth winds.

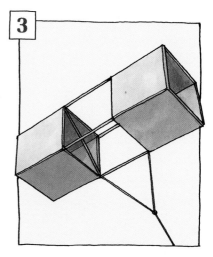

3 Moving the bridle back makes the kite fly at a steeper angle. Use in medium to gusty wind conditions.

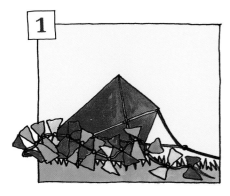

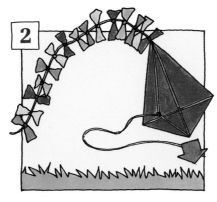

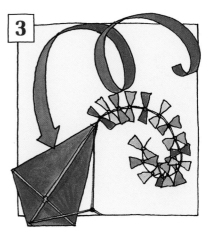

Trouble Shooting

1 Kite fails to rise: not enough wind, bridle too short, or tail too long.

2 Kite flies, then crashes: bridle may need to be shortened.

3 Kite spins or wobbles: add more tail.

Landing your kite

To land your kite, wind in the string on your reel. If the wind is quite strong, try pulling the string in hand over hand until the kite comes down.

DRACULA'S CLOAK

All kinds of simple kites can be made out of paper. Dracula's Cloak can be made out of plain white paper, but it looks much more sinister in purple or black. It flies well in a gentle breeze.

Instead of painting your kite, try cutting shapes out of colored paper and gluing them on the surface with white paste.

1

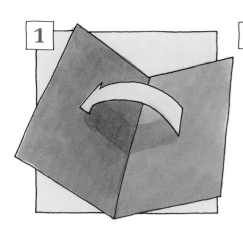

Fold a $11\frac{1}{2}$ x $16\frac{1}{2}$-inch sheet of typing-weight paper carefully across the middle as shown above.

2

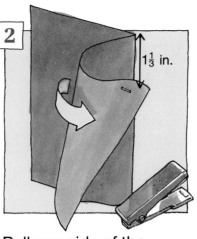

$1\frac{1}{3}$ in.

Pull one side of the sheet around in a curve. Staple it against the center fold, $1\frac{1}{3}$ inches from the tip.

3

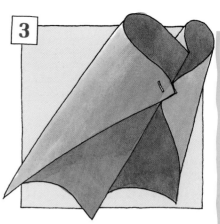

Repeat on the other side. Make sure the corners slightly overlap the center fold, as shown above.

4

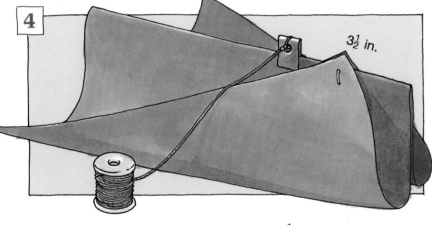

$3\frac{1}{2}$ in.

The Dracula's Cloak kite doesn't need a bridle ring. Just cut a square piece of thick tape and press it on the center

fold, $3\frac{1}{2}$ inches from the tip. Make a hole in the tape as shown in the picture with a hole punch or a pair of scissors.

5

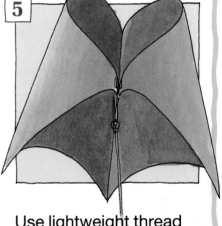

Use lightweight thread to fly the Cloak. It will rise in the lightest breeze and hover menacingly above you!

Dracula's Cloak takes on a bloodthirsty look if you paint some talons, fangs, and a leering face on it. Use felt-tip pens on white paper, and poster paints on colored paper.

6

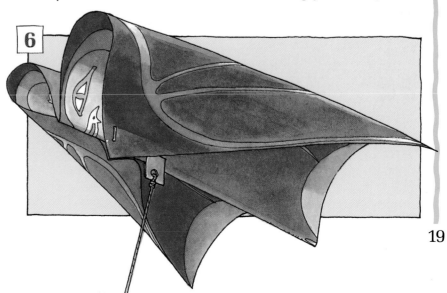

19

TWIN-FIN SKYSLED

Another good flyer in light winds, this kite can be made out of paper or plastic. The one shown here is a good pocket-sized kite, but it could also be made on a larger scale.

Colored tape was used to decorate this Twin-Fin. You could also use bright poster paint.

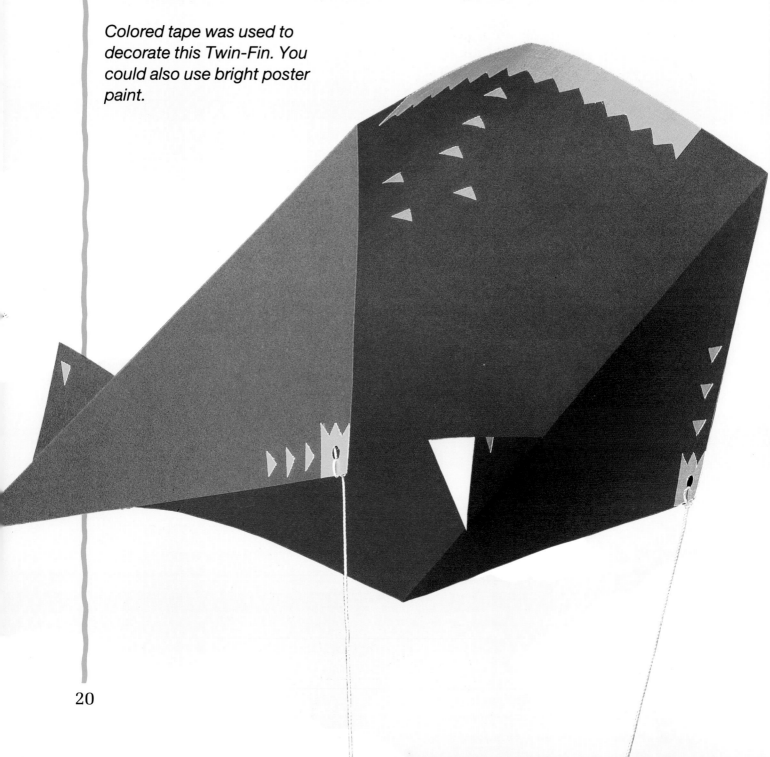

1

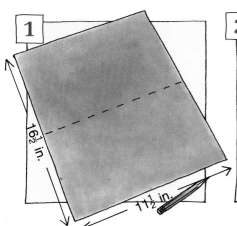

Mark a center line down the middle of a piece of paper $11\frac{1}{2}$ x $16\frac{1}{2}$ inches. Do not fold the sheet, as this will spoil flight performance.

2

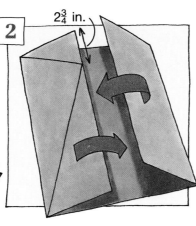

Fold both ends in to the center line. Cut the sides in the triangle pattern shown — the tips should be $2\frac{3}{4}$ inches from the end of the kite.

3

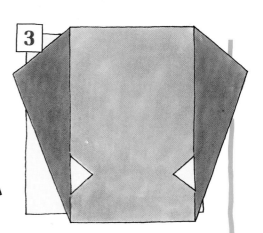

Cut out the two twin-fin stabilizers. Heavy paper fins can be folded up. Plastic ones will flop until they are blown by the wind.

4

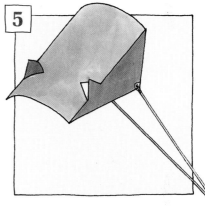

Strengthen the corners to take the strain of the bridle. It is simplest to use strong tape and to make the holes with a hole punch.

5

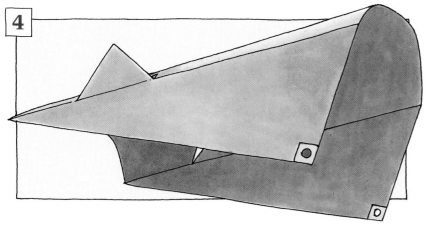

Tie on a long bridle, two to three times the length of the kite. Start with 27 inches, and adjust if necessary.

Use Melinex or shiny wrapping paper to make a kite which dazzles like an alien spacecraft in the sky!

DIAMOND TWO-STICK

The Diamond Two-stick is a classic kite design. The one shown here has two bridle rings — use the top ring in light winds, the bottom one for stronger conditions. Add a longer tail if the kite wobbles in flight.

1

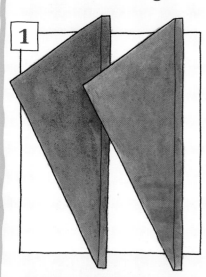

Cut two triangles out of plastic sheeting or rip-stop nylon. Make them the same size, and allow an extra $\frac{3}{8}$-inch overlap on the spine edge.

2

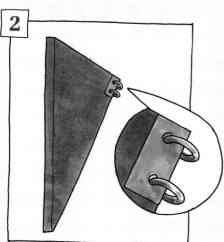

3

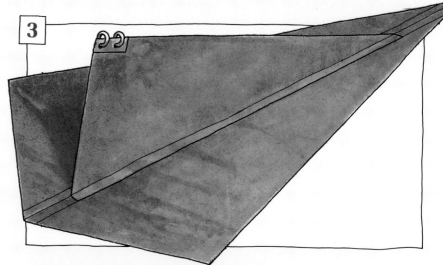

Sew or tape the two sails together. Join them along their longest sides, as shown above. Sew or tape on the fin, positioning it $3\frac{1}{2}$ inches from the tip of the kite.

Cut out a fin, allowing $\frac{3}{8}$-inch overlap. Cover the corner with tape, punch two holes, and slip on two split rings.

4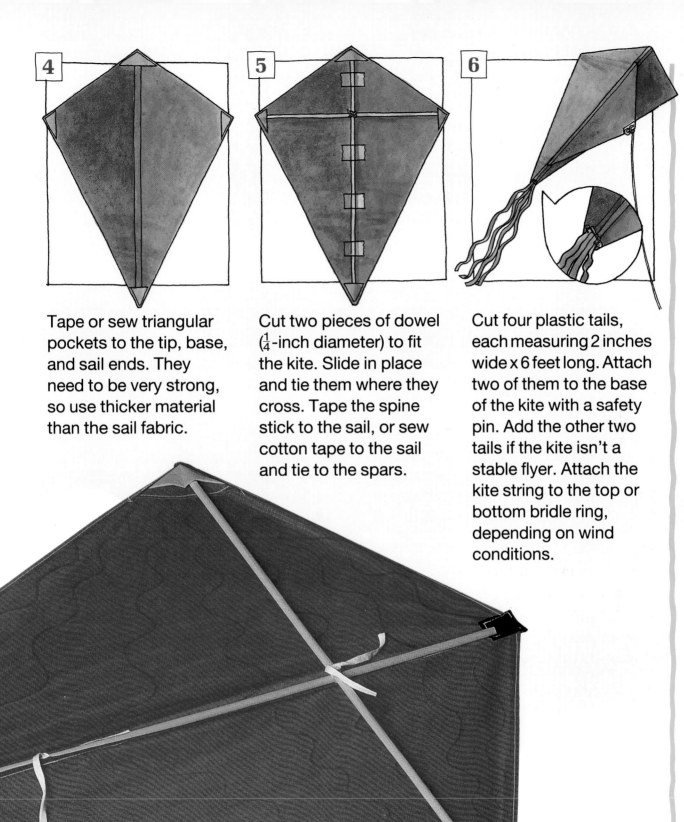

Tape or sew triangular pockets to the tip, base, and sail ends. They need to be very strong, so use thicker material than the sail fabric.

5

Cut two pieces of dowel ($\frac{1}{4}$-inch diameter) to fit the kite. Slide in place and tie them where they cross. Tape the spine stick to the sail, or sew cotton tape to the sail and tie to the spars.

6

Cut four plastic tails, each measuring 2 inches wide x 6 feet long. Attach two of them to the base of the kite with a safety pin. Add the other two tails if the kite isn't a stable flyer. Attach the kite string to the top or bottom bridle ring, depending on wind conditions.

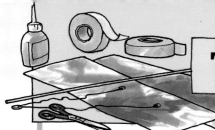

THE RINGWING

This Ringwing was made out of thin cardboard and $\frac{1}{4}$-inch diameter carbon fiber rod. It flies well, but needs a strong wind for a good liftoff.

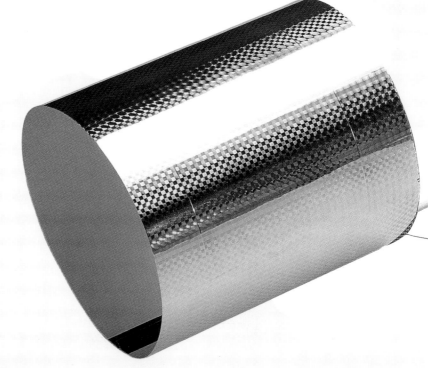

1

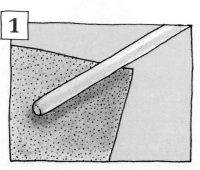

Cut a 36-inch-long piece of dowel or carbon fiber rod. Smooth the ends with sandpaper.

2

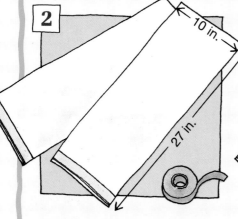

Cut two pieces of thin cardboard, each 10 x 27 inches. Press double-sided tape on one end of each sheet.

3

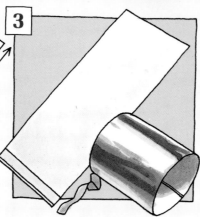

Fold the ends around to form circular sails. Press firmly over the taped edge to make sure it is secure.

4

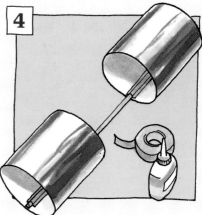

Use white glue to attach each sail to the spar, and tape them in place. Try to make sure the sails are perfectly straight.

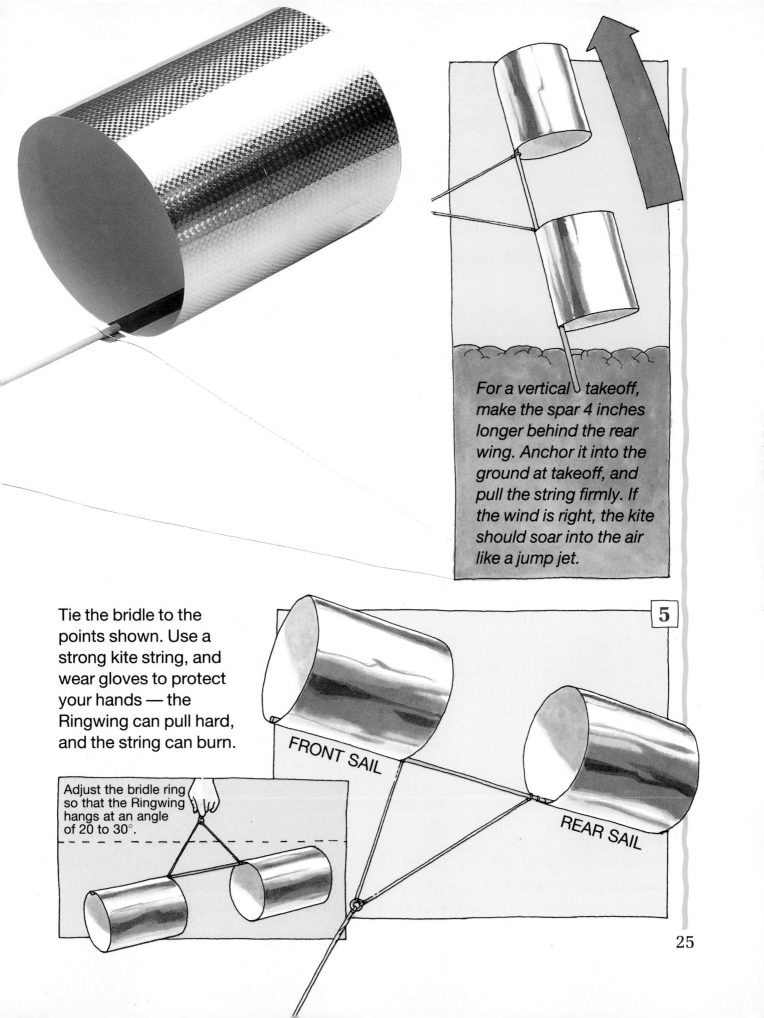

For a vertical takeoff, make the spar 4 inches longer behind the rear wing. Anchor it into the ground at takeoff, and pull the string firmly. If the wind is right, the kite should soar into the air like a jump jet.

Tie the bridle to the points shown. Use a strong kite string, and wear gloves to protect your hands — the Ringwing can pull hard, and the string can burn.

FRONT SAIL

REAR SAIL

Adjust the bridle ring so that the Ringwing hangs at an angle of 20 to 30°.

BOX KITE

The sails of this box kite are made from acoustic tiles. They can be bought in hardware stores, and come in standard sizes — usually 12 inches square. The frame is made from $\frac{1}{4}$-inch diameter wooden dowel.

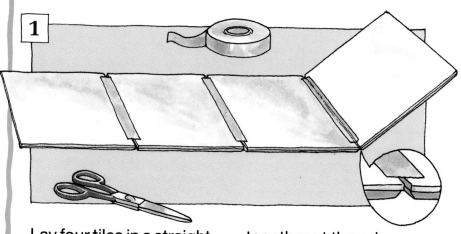

1 Lay four tiles in a straight line on a flat surface. Make sure that the angled edges are face down. Tape the tiles together at the edges. Then fold them into a box shape, and tape together on the inside, as shown below.

2 Make another sail the same way, making sure that the edges are evenly taped.

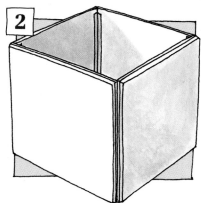

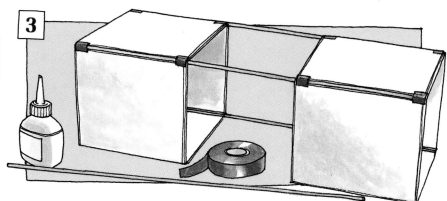

3 Cut the dowels into four spars, each 36 inches long. Glue to the sails with white glue, and hold in place with tape. The spars should fit into the angled corners of the cubes as shown.

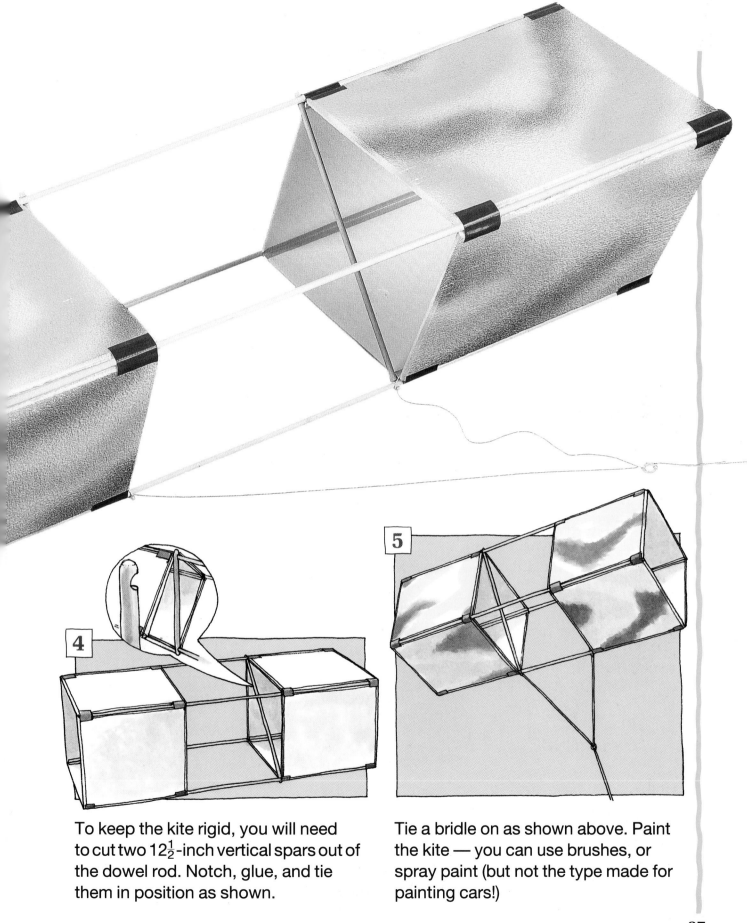

To keep the kite rigid, you will need to cut two $12\frac{1}{2}$-inch vertical spars out of the dowel rod. Notch, glue, and tie them in position as shown.

Tie a bridle on as shown above. Paint the kite — you can use brushes, or spray paint (but not the type made for painting cars!)

THE BLACK MAMBA

The sight of the Mamba slithering across the sky is enough to send a shiver down the strongest spine — yet it's little more than a cleverly sliced plastic garbage bag.

1

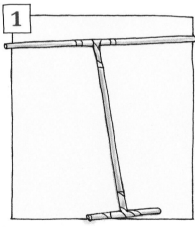

Cut three lengths of $\frac{1}{8}$-inch diameter plastic rod to make a T-shape, as shown in the diagram. Fasten the three rods together with tape.

2

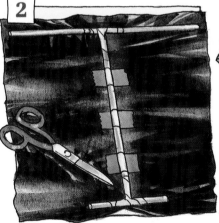

Cut open a black plastic garbage bag, and lay the frame on top. Tape the spine and base. Trim the plastic, leaving $\frac{3}{4}$ inch at the top and bottom.

3

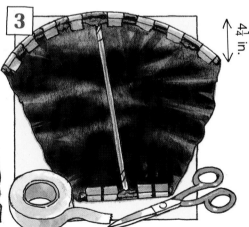

$4\frac{1}{4}$ in.

Bend down the top rod so that the ends are $4\frac{1}{4}$ inches below the tip. Tape the plastic securely, and trim the sides as shown.

Cut sinister features from colored paper or plastic and glue them on the Mamba's face.

4

Tape the edges — this adds strength to the kite and prevents it from ripping in strong winds, or when it is coming in to land.

5

Cut the rest of the bag into 6-inch-wide strips. Tape them together to make a long tail, and cut the end into a point. Tape the flat edge to the base of the kite. Make two holes as shown, and tie on a bridle — adjust it if you need to improve the Mamba's flight.

THE SUPERSTUNTER

Take command of the air with this twin-line kite! The two lines let you climb, dive, spin, and soar, but be warned — the Superstunter is a nervous flyer, and the slightest mistake will send it hurtling to the ground.

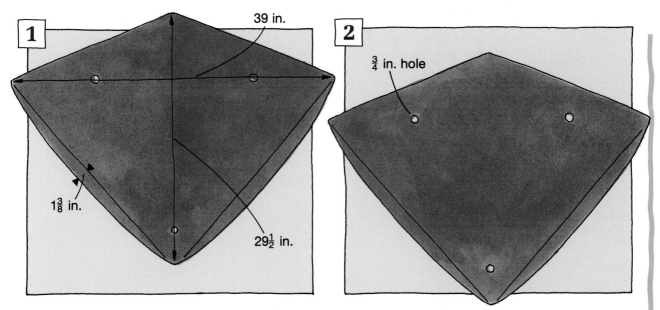

1

39 in.

$1\frac{3}{8}$ in.

$29\frac{1}{2}$ in.

2

$\frac{3}{4}$ in. hole

Draw this sail plan on a large sheet of paper to the sizes shown. Cut out, and pin to a sheet of plastic. Cut out the plastic sail.

Make three holes, $\frac{3}{4}$ inch across, for the bridle. Then tape a plastic pocket (buy these from a kite store, or make your own) into each corner.

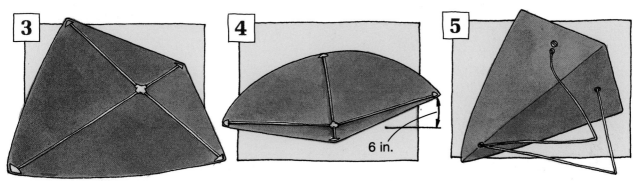

3

4

6 in.

5

Cut four pieces of $\frac{1}{4}$-inch dowel to fit the sail. Put into a metal joint, and slip the ends into the pockets.

To make the angled wing, keep one wing flat on your work surface and bend up the other wing.

Two bridles are used for this kite. Tie them to the spars through the holes, as shown above.

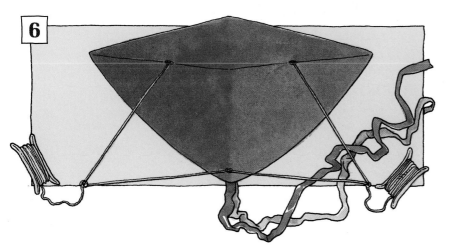

6

Tie on the bridle rings, and tie to two separate kite strings. Make tails by cutting old plastic bags into streamers and taping them to the base of the kite.

DELTA STAR

Use adhesive shapes as a quick way of decorating your Delta.

This classic design flies in light winds and is very stable. It can be made from plastic and tape or sewn in ripstop nylon like the one shown here. Add long pennants and streamers for extra interest.

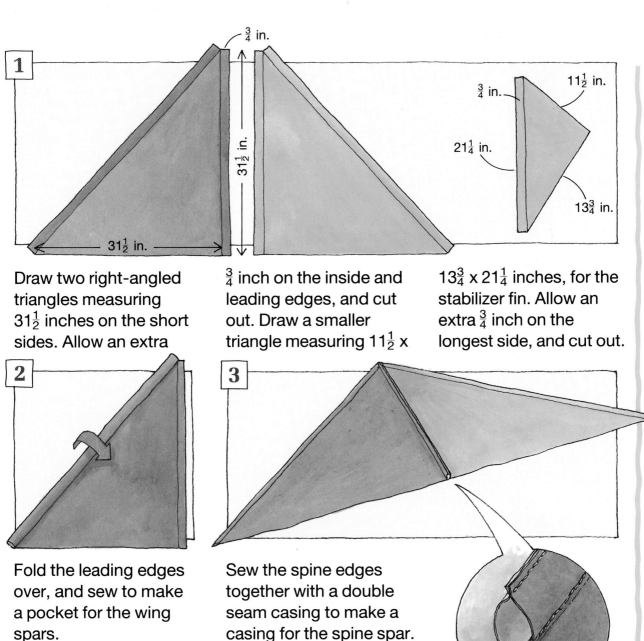

1

$\frac{3}{4}$ in.

$31\frac{1}{2}$ in.

$31\frac{1}{2}$ in.

$\frac{3}{4}$ in.

$11\frac{1}{2}$ in.

$21\frac{1}{4}$ in.

$13\frac{3}{4}$ in.

Draw two right-angled triangles measuring $31\frac{1}{2}$ inches on the short sides. Allow an extra

$\frac{3}{4}$ inch on the inside and leading edges, and cut out. Draw a smaller triangle measuring $11\frac{1}{2}$ x

$13\frac{3}{4}$ x $21\frac{1}{4}$ inches, for the stabilizer fin. Allow an extra $\frac{3}{4}$ inch on the longest side, and cut out.

2

Fold the leading edges over, and sew to make a pocket for the wing spars.

3

Sew the spine edges together with a double seam casing to make a casing for the spine spar.

4

Attach the fin to the spine as shown by sewing down the side of

the spine spar casing. Sew a bridle ring pocket to the fin (see page 9).

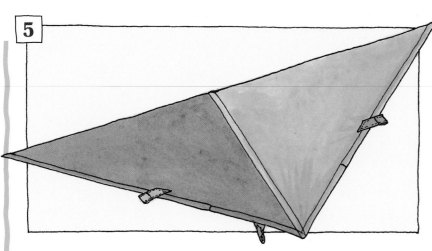

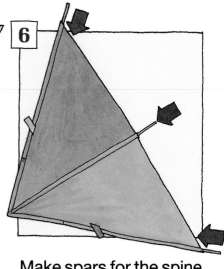

Make two pockets for the cross-brace spar. Sew the pockets to the leading edges, as shown on page 9. Make sure that the pockets are positioned 20 inches from the tip of the kite.

Make spars for the spine and leading edges from $\frac{1}{4}$-inch dowel cut into 8-inch lengths.

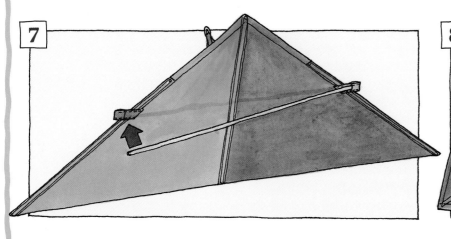

Cut another piece of $\frac{1}{4}$-inch dowel $31\frac{1}{2}$ inches long. This is the cross-brace spar. Slip the ends of the spar into the two pockets you have attached to the leading edges of the kite.

If you like, cut a scalloped edge along the base of the Delta, as shown above.

Decorate the Delta with adhesive stars, and attach tails to the base. You could also add a tailspinner (page 14), or even tie on a banner with a message!

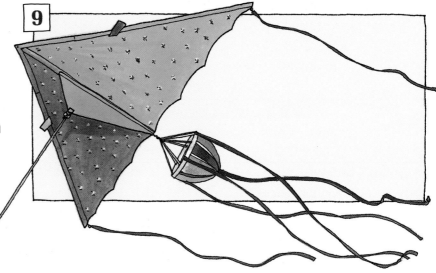

HEXAFRINGE

The design for this six-sided kite comes from Greece, a land of sea and sunshine. On a sunny day, the kite's many-colored fringe and long tail make it one of the prettiest you are likely to see. To make it, you will need to do some drilling — ask an adult to help you.

1

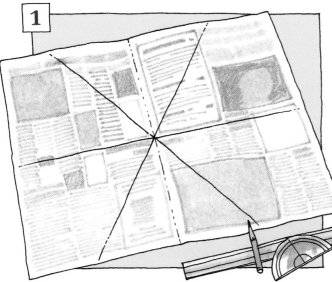

Draw the pattern shown above on a large sheet of newspaper. Use a protractor to make each angle measure 60°.

Cut $\frac{1}{4}$-inch-square wooden sticks into three $31\frac{1}{2}$-inch lengths. Smooth the ends with sandpaper. Using a very small drill bit, make a hole $\frac{1}{8}$ inch from the end of each stick.

Tape the sticks to the pattern, one on top of the other. Make sure that the holes are on the sides. Then firmly tie the sticks in the middle with twine. Remove the pattern.

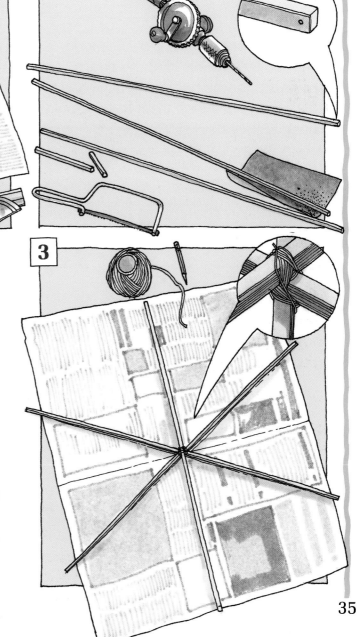

4

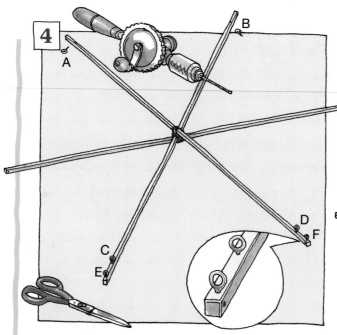

Drill four more holes, A, B, C, and D, 2 inches from the end of the spars. These are for the bridles. Finally, drill holes E and F, $\frac{3}{8}$ inch from the ends. These are for the tail. Screw eyehooks into all these six holes.

5

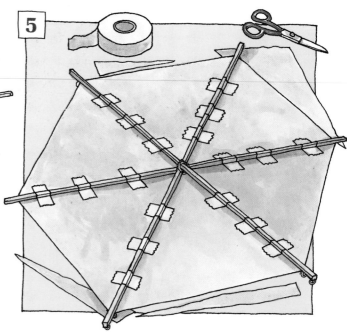

Tape the spars firmly to a large sheet of brown wrapping paper with the eyehooks pointing down. Cut the paper into a hexagonal sail, as shown — the spars must be 2 inches longer than the sail.

6

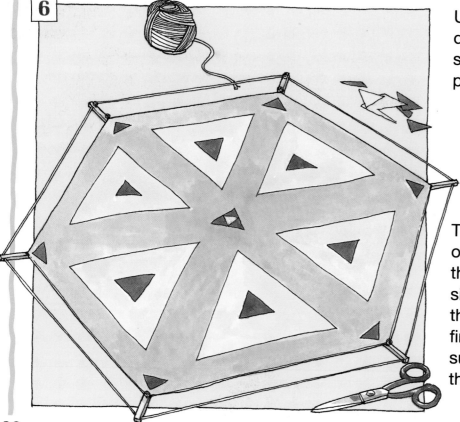

Use poster paint to decorate the sail, or glue shapes cut from colored paper.

Thread a long length of fishing line or strong thread through the side holes at the end of the spars, and tie firmly. This line supports the fringe of the kite.

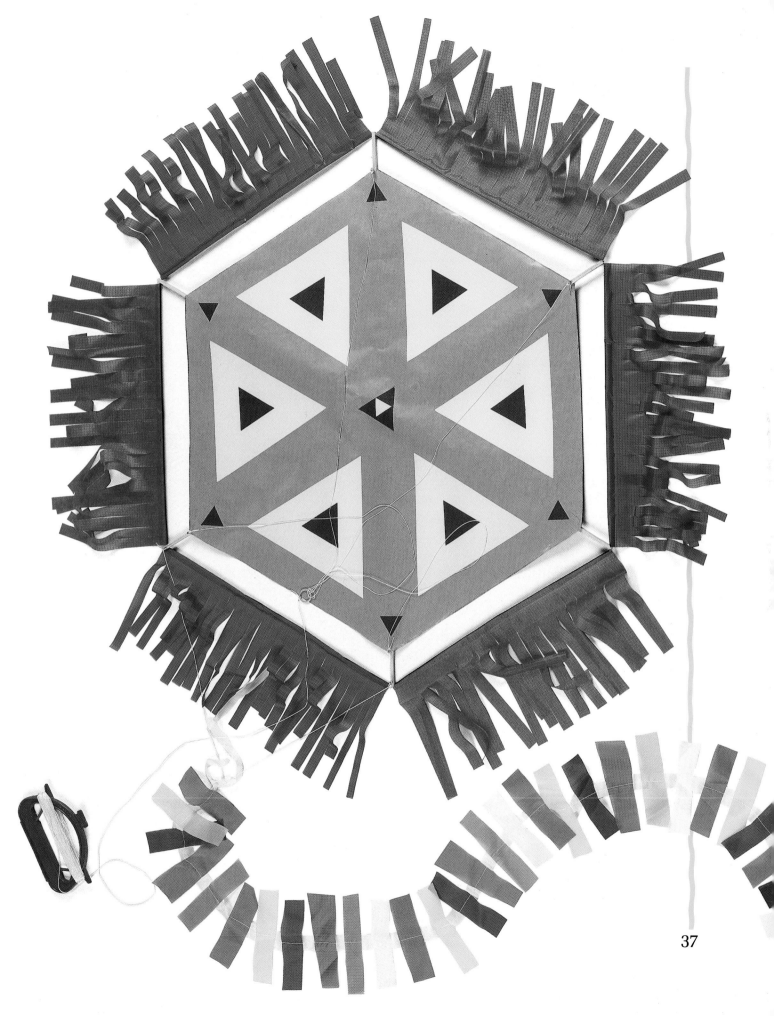

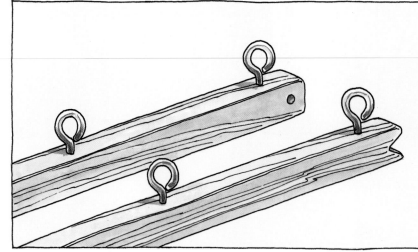

Holes and Notches

As an alternative to drilling holes for the fringe, you could try cutting V-shaped notches at the end of each spar with a craft knife. As with drilling, always ask an adult to help you.

7

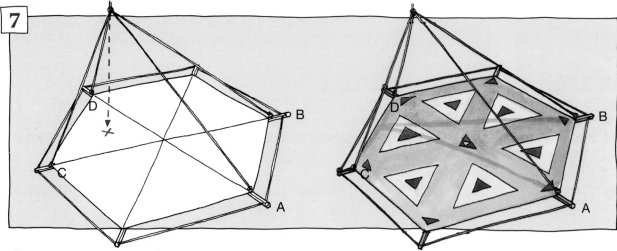

Cut four pieces of kite string for the bridle. Tie one end of a piece of string to each eyehook (marked A, B, C, and D). Then tie the free ends to a bridle ring. You will need to adjust the length of each bridle line, so that when the kite is held by the bridle ring, the four lines meet at a point directly above and in the middle of points C and D (see the diagram above).

Cut two more pieces of string, and tie them to the eyehooks E and F. Tie them together so that the lines run parallel to the edges of the kite.

8

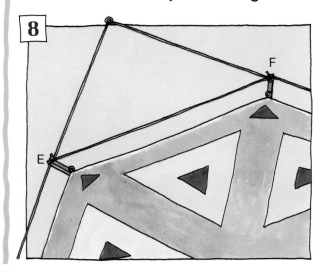

Make a tail from pieces of colored plastic — shopping bags are ideal. Try 3 yards to begin with — you may need to add more later.

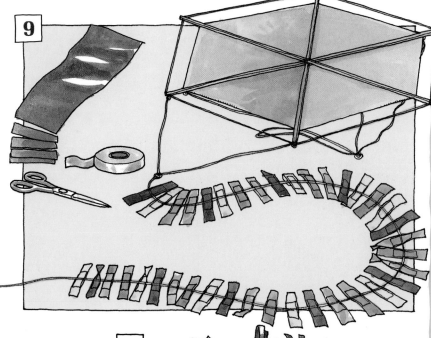

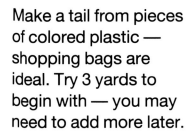

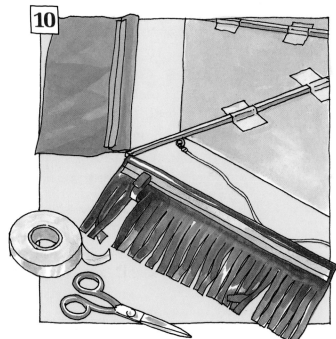

Make a fringe out of plastic or paper. Cut six strips, about 3 inches wide and the same length as the sides of the kite. Fold them over the edge threads, tape in place, and cut a fringe.

The Hexafringe likes a steady breeze best of all. It is a good climber and in a strong wind will rise as fast as you can play out the string.

MORE IDEAS

Once you feel confident about making kites, you might like to try designing your own. In the meantime, here are a few more ideas for you to consider....

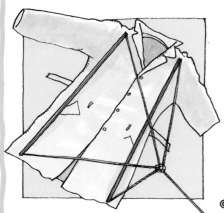

All you need is a thin plastic raincoat (the kind that folds into a pocket), and two wooden spars!

Based on ancient Chinese designs, this flying fish is little more than a decorated wind sock.

Tie balloons to the ends of poles, and use stunt kites to try to burst them. It's harder than you might think.

This tiny kite is only 1 inch across, but it can fly in front of a mini fan. Use very light sail material.

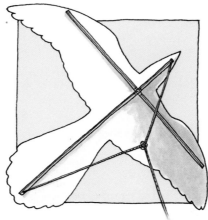

Kites in the shape of birds are fun. A prehistoric version could be made in the shape of a pterosaur.

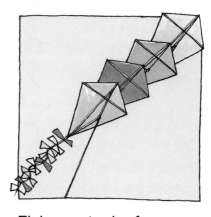

Flying a stack of matching kites is a popular sport. The stable Delta kite is well suited to stacking.